I0797409

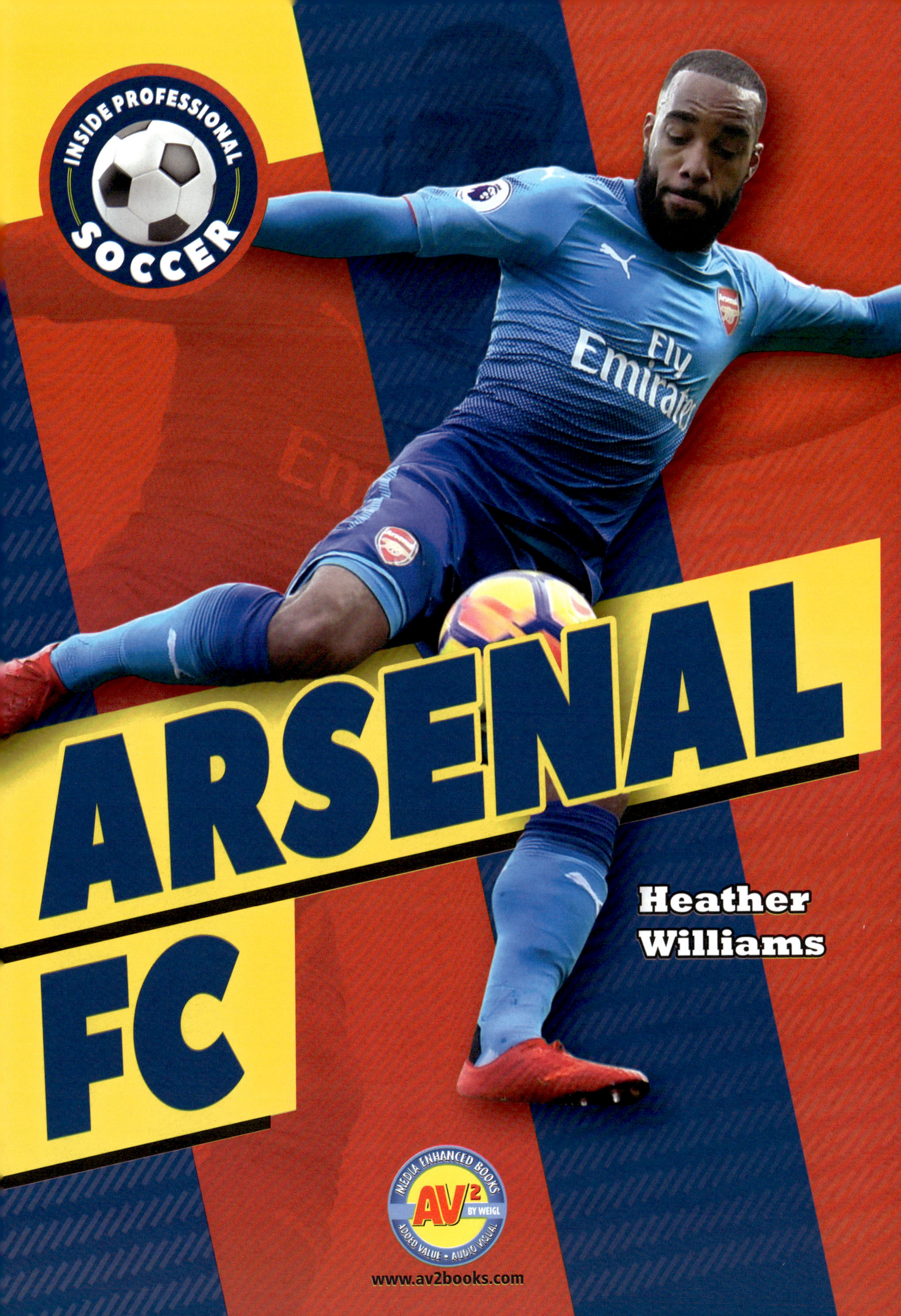
INSIDE PROFESSIONAL
SOCCER
Fly Emirates
ARSENAL
FC
Heather
Williams
MEDIA ENHANCED BOOKS
AV2
BY WEIGL
ADDED VALUE • AUDIO VISUAL
www.av2books.com

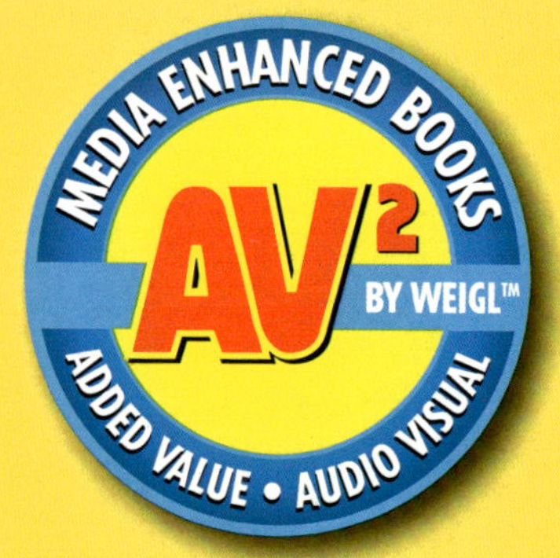

Go to **www.av2books.com**, and enter this book's unique code.

BOOK CODE

AVP96525

AV² by Weigl brings you media enhanced books that support active learning.

AV² provides enriched content that supplements and complements this book. Weigl's AV² books strive to create inspired learning and engage young minds in a total learning experience.

Your AV² Media Enhanced books come alive with...

Audio
Listen to sections of the book read aloud.

Key Words
Study vocabulary, and complete a matching word activity.

Video
Watch informative video clips.

Quizzes
Test your knowledge.

Embedded Weblinks
Gain additional information for research.

Slide Show
View images and captions, and prepare a presentation.

Try This!
Complete activities and hands-on experiments.

... and much, much more!

Published by AV² by Weigl
350 5th Avenue, 59th Floor
New York, NY 10118
Website: www.av2books.com

Library of Congress Control Number: 2018930409

ISBN 978-1-4896-7781-5 (hardcover)
ISBN 978-1-4896-7782-2 (softcover)
ISBN 978-1-4896-7783-9 (multi-user eBook)

Printed in the United States of America in Brainerd, Minnesota
1 2 3 4 5 6 7 8 9 0 22 21 20 19 18

022018
120817

Project Coordinator: John Willis   Designer: Terry Paulhus

The publisher acknowledges Getty Images and Alamy as its primary image suppliers for this title.

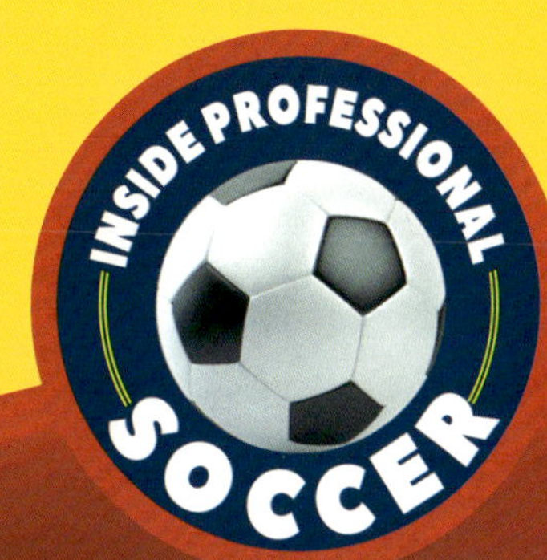

CONTENTS

AV² Book Code 2
Introduction 4
History 6
The Arena 8
Where They Play 10
The Uniforms 12
Goalie Gear 14
The Coaches 16
Fans Around the World 18
Legends of the Past 20
Stars of Today 22
All-Time Records 24
Timeline 26
Write a Biography 28
Trivia Time 30
Key Words/Index 31
www.av2books.com 32

Introduction

London, England, is known for its history, culture, and arts. It is also known for its professional soccer. Soccer is called football in most European countries. Millions of people fill stadiums in London to watch soccer matches each year. Billions more around the world watch their favorite teams online and on television.

Arsenal Football **Club** is one of the most popular soccer teams in Great Britain. Arsenal is part of Great Britain's **Premier League**. The Premier League is the most watched sports league in the world. It ranks third in income behind the National Football League (NFL) and Major League Baseball (MLB).

Star player Alexis Sánchez is originally from Chile. He has been playing with Arsenal since 2014.

Arsenal was the first London soccer team to turn professional. The team has also won nearly 50 championship **titles** and **cups**. Arsenal played in the first football match ever shown on live television. The team's history, success on the field, and world-class stadium make Arsenal worthy of a closer look.

In 2017, striker Alexandre Lacazette became the first Arsenal player since 1988 to score in his first three league games.

ARSENAL FC

Arena Emirates Stadium

Division Premier League

Head Coach Arsène Wenger

Location London, England

FIFA Club World Cups 0

Nicknames The Gunners

18 Players with 100-plus goals

5 Home stadiums

13 Football Association Challenge (FA) Cup Wins

45 Total trophies

60,161 Record Home Attendance

History

Arsenal won its first FA Cup in 1930, led by Jack Lambert and Alex James.

In the winter of 1886, several factory workers from Woolwich, London, England, decided to form a soccer club. They called themselves Dial Square, after a sundial on the Royal Arsenal factory where they worked. The next month, they changed the team's name to Royal Arsenal. Once the team turned professional, they changed their name again, to Woolwich Arsenal. Today, the team is known simply as Arsenal.

In 1913, two businessmen, named Henry Norris and William Hall, invested in the club. They moved Arsenal to a new stadium in Highbury, London. Norris and Hall also hired a new coach in 1925. His name was Herbert Chapman. Chapman transformed Arsenal into a championship team. The team won a national cup and two league trophies in just three years.

Arsenal did not win a single trophy from 1953 to 1970. Things started to change for the team during the 1970–1971 season. Arsenal earned two major titles, the Premier League and the FA Cup, in what is known as a double. In 1986, a former Arsenal player, named George Graham, became coach. He led the team to several titles. Current coach Arsène Wenger was hired in 1996. His leadership has resulted in nearly 20 trophies for Arsenal.

In the 1971 FA Cup final, Arsenal scored twice in extra time to win the game.

The Arena

When Emirates Stadium opened in 2006, Queen Elizabeth II was not feeling well. Prince Philip attended in her place to officially open the stadium.

Originally called Gillespie Road, the subway station near the stadium was renamed Arsenal, after the team, in 1932.

Arsenal played at Highbury Stadium for 93 years. The team moved to its new home **pitch**, called Emirates Stadium, in 2006. Emirates is the fifth-largest soccer stadium in Great Britain. It holds more than 60,000 people.

Emirates Stadium honors the time Arsenal spent at Highbury in many ways. Several statues from Highbury were moved to the new stadium. The giant clock that once hung at Highbury now hangs at the entrance of Emirates. The seating sections also have the same names as those in the old stadium.

The club updated Emirates Stadium three years after it opened. They called this update "Arsenalization." They wanted to make Emirates look like it truly belonged to Arsenal. This included adding large paintings, known as murals, around the stadium. Some of the murals are of legendary players from the team. Other murals show important moments from the club's history. Several statues of important players have also been placed outside the stadium. Two bridges leading into the stadium are named after former Arsenal directors Ken Friar and Danny Fiszman.

"The Spirit of Highbury" is a large mural that includes a photo of every player who played for Arsenal between 1913 and 2006.

Where They Play

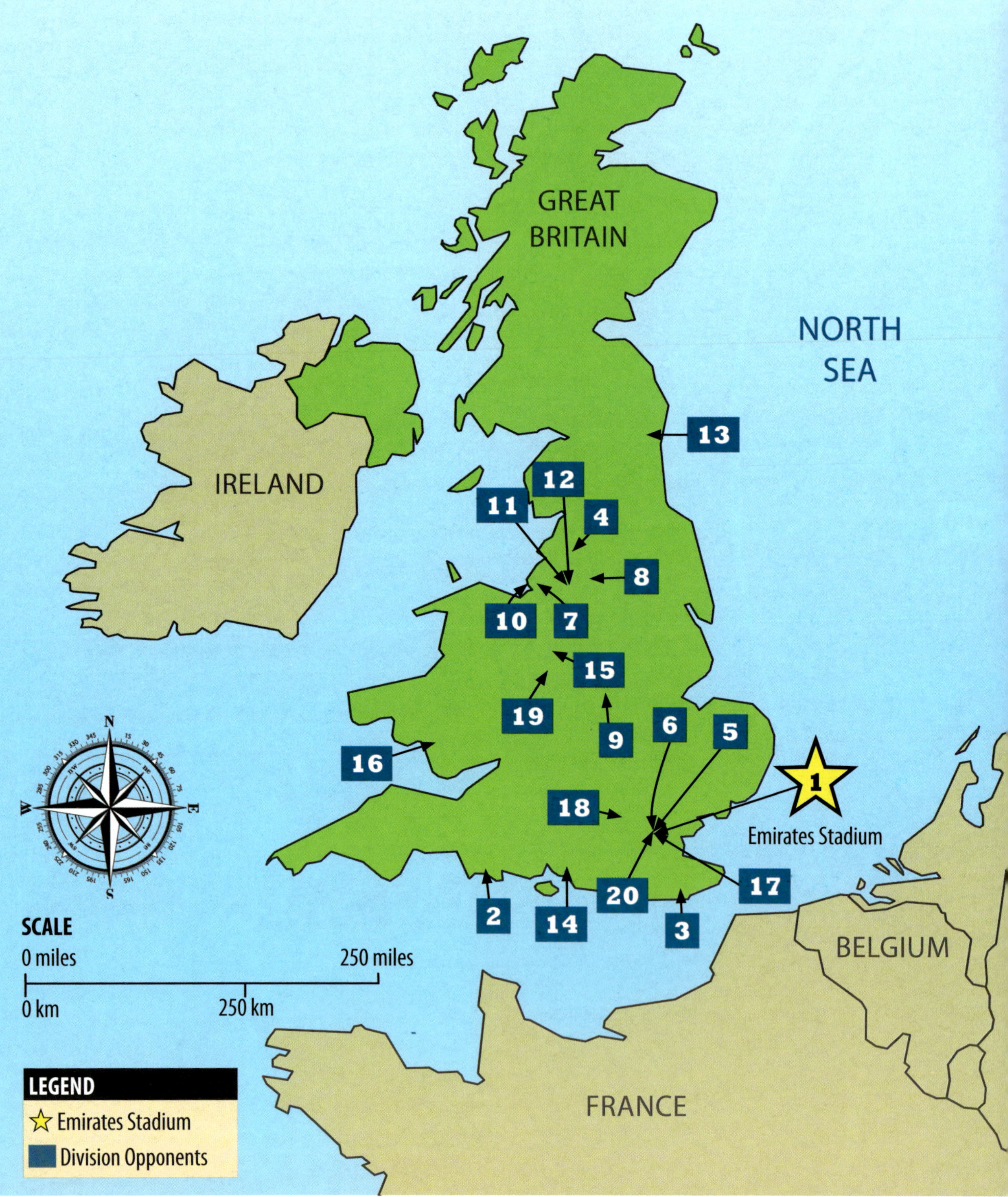

SWEDEN

FINLAND

NORWAY

DENMARK

GERMANY

Arena
Emirates Stadium

Location
Holloway, London, England

Broke Ground
2004

Completed
2006

Field Design
The stadium is constructed of many steel beams and glass panels to give the illusion that it glistens in the sunlight and glows at night.

Features

- In one part of the stadium, a group of white seats forms the picture of the cannon from Arsenal's logo
- 2,222 premium box seats (boxes cost up to $13,000 per game, with food, drinks, leather reclining seats, and private waiters)
- Four statues highlighting important figures in Arsenal history were unveiled in 2009

PREMIER LEAGUE TEAMS

★ 1 Arsenal *(Highbury, London, England)*
2 Bournemouth *(Bournemouth, England)*
3 Brighton and Hove Albion *(Brighton and Hove, England)*
4 Burnley *(Burnley, England)*
5 Chelsea *(West London, England)*
6 Crystal Palace *(South London, England)*
7 Everton *(Liverpool, England)*
8 Huddersfield Town *(Huddersfield, England)*
9 Leicester City *(Leicester, England)*
10 Liverpool *(Liverpool, England)*
11 Manchester City *(Manchester, England)*
12 Manchester United *(Manchester, England)*
13 Newcastle United *(Newcastle upon Tyne, England)*
14 Southampton *(Southampton, England)*
15 Stoke City *(Stoke-on-Trent, England)*
16 Swansea City *(Swansea, Wales)*
17 Tottenham Hotspur *(North London, England)*
18 Watford *(Watford, England)*
19 West Bromwich Albion *(West Bromwich, England)*
20 West Ham United *(East London, England)*

The Uniforms

Arsenal's home uniform has not changed much since 1925, when coach Herbert Chapman added white sleeves to the red jersey.

In 1886, when Arsenal was formed, the team coaches were unable to afford uniforms for the players. Two of the players asked their former team, Nottingham Forest, for some old **kits**. Nottingham's old red shirts became Arsenal's home colors.

The away uniform colors date back to the early years of the team. When playing Nottingham, Arsenal needed a different color. They played in a shirt with blue and white stripes. Yellow was introduced in 1970. In 1971, the team won a championship wearing yellow shirts.

Arsenal's logo is a red crest with blue stripes on either side. It is edged in gold and features a gold cannon in the center. "Arsenal" is written in white above the cannon. The logo pays tribute to the club's origins, as well as the team's nickname, "The Gunners."

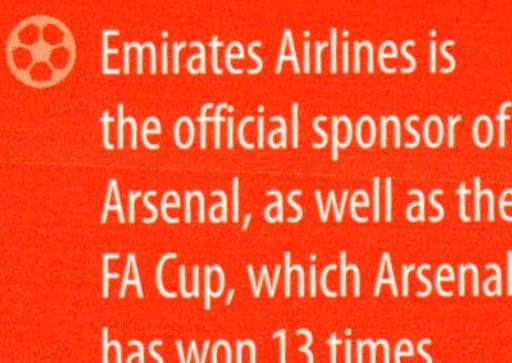

Emirates Airlines is the official sponsor of Arsenal, as well as the FA Cup, which Arsenal has won 13 times.

Goalie Gear

Safety awareness is becoming more important for goalies, who often collide with other players and the goal during big saves.

Goalkeepers must stand out from field players and field officials. Goalies usually wear long sleeves and brightly colored jerseys. They can wear pants, rather than shorts, if they choose. Most wear special goalkeeping gloves. These gloves have rubbery surfaces to help them grip the ball. Some goalkeeper gloves contain plastic spines to protect their hands from injuries.

Arsenal's goalkeeper is Petr Čech. He often wears hunter green, bright yellow, or turquoise. Čech also wears a protective helmet because of a head injury. In 2006, Čech played in a match against Reading. During the first minute, he collided with an opposing player's knee. His skull was severely fractured. Čech has no long-term effects from the injury. However, he continues to play in a helmet.

Petr Čech's original helmet was made by Canterbury of New Zealand, but since Adidas made Arsenal's uniforms, the company developed a special helmet of their own for him.

The Coaches

Arsenal head coach Arséne Wenger's insistence on healthy eating for his team was inspired by his two years in Japan, where he noticed that people ate mostly fish and vegetables and avoided sugar and fat.

Arsenal has been coached by 25 different coaches. Of those, 7 were temporary. The other 18 were permanent. Sam Hollis is often referred to as the club's first coach. However, he was actually the team trainer. Thomas Mitchell was Arsenal's first professional coach. Arsenal's most successful coach is current coach Arsène Wenger.

ARSÈNE WENGER Arsène Wenger is Arsenal's longest serving coach. Wenger's nickname is "The Professor" because he is very serious. Wenger began coaching Arsenal in 1996. At this time, he focused on health and fitness. He created a healthy eating plan and gave players vitamins. He also started strict training sessions. Wenger has led Arsenal to 17 titles, including 7 national titles.

HERBERT CHAPMAN Herbert Chapman is considered one of Great Britain's greatest soccer coaches of all time. Chapman was a strong believer in physical fitness. He hired **physiotherapists** and massage therapists for the team. Chapman also added floodlights to Highbury Stadium so the team could play at night. He led the team to its first league championship in the 1930–1931 season.

BERTIE MEE Bertie Mee was so uncertain about becoming Arsenal's head coach that his contract included an **escape clause**. He was originally the team's physiotherapist. Mee ended up leading Arsenal to its first trophy win in 17 years. He coached from 1966 to 1976. Mee became Arsenal's most winning coach, with 241 wins. He held that record until it was broken by Wenger.

Fans Around the World

Arsenal has around 100 million fans worldwide who watch games on TV and online, and who interact with players and other fans on social media.

Arsenal fans refer to themselves as "Gooners" because it sounds like the team's nickname, "The Gunners." Some fan groups include the Arsenal Football Supporters Club and REDaction. Arsenal's fan base is the fifth-largest group of soccer fans in the world. Arsenal fans are very active on social media. The team has more than 37 million Facebook followers and nearly 13 million Twitter followers. There is even an Arsenal app that gives updates on player statistics and game information.

Fan groups design and hang banners around the stadium before each match. Fans also join together during matches to sing "One Nil to the Arsenal." Fan groups publish blogs about the team. They also publish fan magazines such as *The Gooner* and *Gunflash*.

Fan Traditions

#1 Traditional English meat pies are a pre-game staple. One restaurant near Emirates Stadium has pies named after Arsenal legends. These include "The Ian Wright" and "The Thierry Henry."

#2 A large "49" flag was designed by a local graphic artist and Gunners fan. It represents Arsenal's 49-league-game winning streak. It is passed around the lower seating area before matches.

Legends of the Past

Many great players have suited up for Arsenal FC. A few of them have become icons of the team and the city it represents.

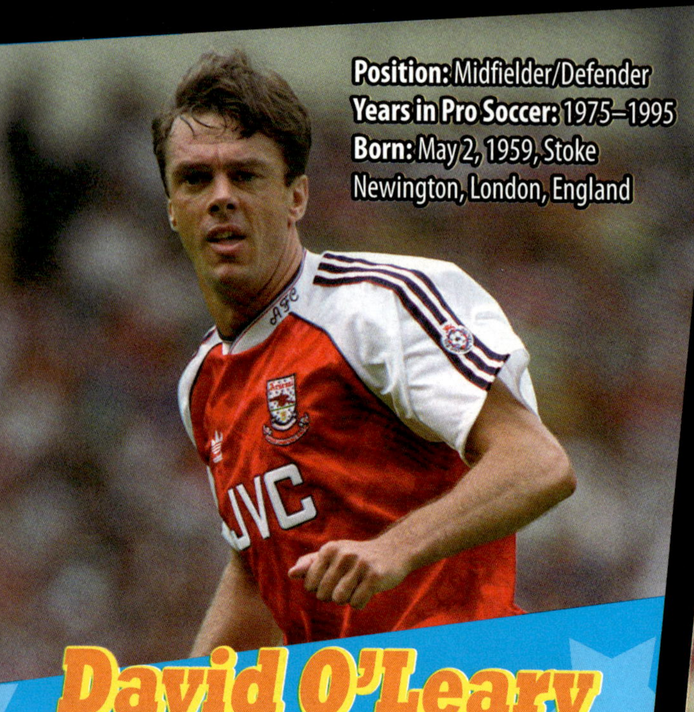

Position: Midfielder/Defender
Years in Pro Soccer: 1975–1995
Born: May 2, 1959, Stoke Newington, London, England

David O'Leary

David O'Leary spent most of his professional soccer career at Arsenal. He was a key **defender** from 1975 to 1993. O'Leary holds the record for most appearances with Arsenal. He won eight trophies in nearly 20 years with the club. O'Leary also played for the Irish national team. He took the final penalty kick in a shootout against Romania in the 1990 World Cup. It resulted in a win for Ireland. This shot is considered the greatest moment in Irish football. O'Leary went on to manage three club teams, most recently the Shabab Al Ahli Club in Dubai.

Thierry Henry

Thierry Henry made his mark on professional soccer when he joined Arsenal. His former Monaco coach, Arsène Wenger, recruited him. Henry played for Arsenal for eight seasons. He was considered the team's greatest weapon during that time. Henry was a member of the French national team from 1997 to 2010. He played on the 1998 FIFA World Cup championship team. After he retired, Henry became an assistant coach for the Belgian national team.

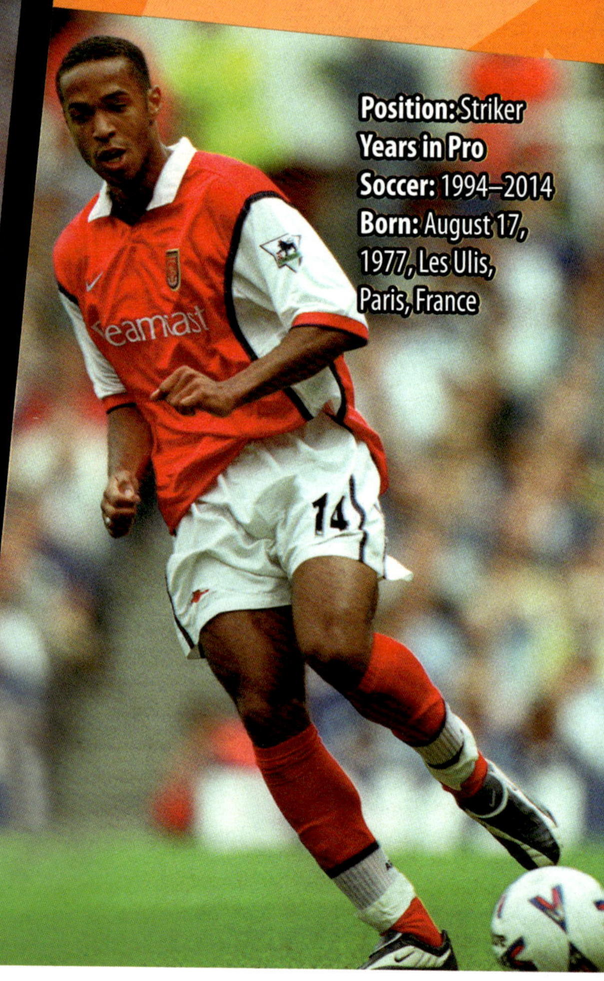

Position: Striker
Years in Pro Soccer: 1994–2014
Born: August 17, 1977, Les Ulis, Paris, France

Pat Jennings

Before signing with Arsenal, Pat Jennings was goalkeeper for Arsenal's biggest local rival, Tottenham Hotspur. His Tottenham coach let him transfer. He did not think Jennings would play soccer much longer. However, Jennings played in 327 games for Arsenal over eight seasons. He was skilled at judging where the ball would enter the net. This helped him make many saves throughout his career. Jennings was a member of the Northern Ireland National Team. He played in seven World Cup matches. Jennings is one of only 21 professional soccer players to make more than 1,000 career game appearances. He played his last official match at the age of 40.

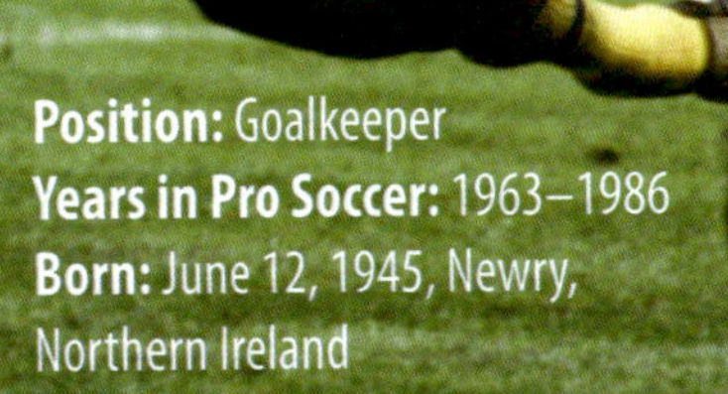

Position: Goalkeeper
Years in Pro Soccer: 1963–1986
Born: June 12, 1945, Newry, Northern Ireland

Ian Wright

Ian Wright is Arsenal's second-highest goal-scorer of all time, with 185 goals. He spent seven seasons with the team. Wright won five trophies with Arsenal, including the Premier League title. He also played 33 matches for the English national team. Wright spent one season as a coach for a small club team. Then, he became a sports television and radio personality. Two of Wright's sons are also professional soccer players.

Position: Striker
Years in Pro Soccer: 1985–2000
Born: November 3, 1963, Woolwich, London, England

Stars of Today

Today's Arsenal FC team is made up of many young, talented players who have proven that they are among the best in the league.

Héctor Bellerín

Héctor Bellerín started playing professional soccer at age 19. He is considered one of the fastest soccer players in the world. Bellerín's speed makes him a major threat to other teams. He is also able to out-dribble many opponents. His ability to outrun other players makes him a powerful defender. Bellerín has made three international appearances with the Spanish national team. He has won two Premier League titles with Arsenal.

Position: Defender
Years in Pro Soccer: 2013–present
Born: March 19, 1995, Barcelona, Spain

Theo Walcott

Theo Walcott has spent most of his professional soccer career as a **forward** for Arsenal. He is best known for his speed and scoring ability, with more than 100 goals for Arsenal. Walcott has won five titles with Arsenal. Three of those titles are Premier League championships. He has made 47 appearances and scored eight goals for the English national team since 2006. Off the soccer field, Walcott is a published children's author. He has written four soccer-themed books.

Position: Forward
Years in Pro Soccer: 2005–present
Born: March 16, 1989, Middlesex, England

Per Mertesacker

Per Mertesacker is one of the most intimidating defenders in professional soccer. He is known for being very tall. Mertesacker stands at 6 feet, 6 inches (198 centimeters). He started playing club soccer at age 11. Mertesacker played for two clubs in Germany before joining Arsenal in 2011. He has played in 216 matches and scored nine goals for Arsenal. Mertesacker was also a member of the German national team from 2004 to 2014. He led Germany to a win in the 2014 FIFA World Cup.

Position: Defender
Years in Pro Soccer: 2003–present
Born: September 29, 1984, Hanover, Germany

Alexis Sánchez

Alexis Sánchez is known as *El Niño Maravilla*, or "Boy Wonder." Sánchez has earned double-digit goals and assists every season he has played with Arsenal. He was named Arsenal's Player of the Year during his first season with the club. Sánchez has scored more than 80 goals with Arsenal. He helped the team win the league championship in 2015 and 2017. Sánchez has also been part of the Chilean national team since 2006. He has scored 38 goals in 115 matches for Chile.

Position: Forward
Years in Pro Soccer: 2005–present
Born: December 19, 1988, Tocopilla, Chile

All-Time Records

13
League Championships
Arsenal boasts 13 Premier League championships, the third highest in British professional football.

49
Win Streak
Between May 2003 and August 2004, Arsenal played 49 straight league matches without a single loss.

228
Goals
Thierry Henry scored a record-high 228 goals for Arsenal.

772
Games Played
David O'Leary's 772 total appearances between 1975 and 1993 is an Arsenal record.

73,707
Fans in Attendance
At a 1998 UEFA match played at Wembley Stadium, in which Arsenal was the home team, a record 73,707 fans were in attendance.

Throughout the team's history, Arsenal FC has had many memorable events that have become defining moments for the team and its fans.

1886
Arsenal is founded in 1886 as Dial Square.

1913
The Gunners move from the Manor Ground to Highbury Arsenal Stadium.

1937
A match between Arsenal's first team and reserve team is the first soccer match ever to be shown on live television.

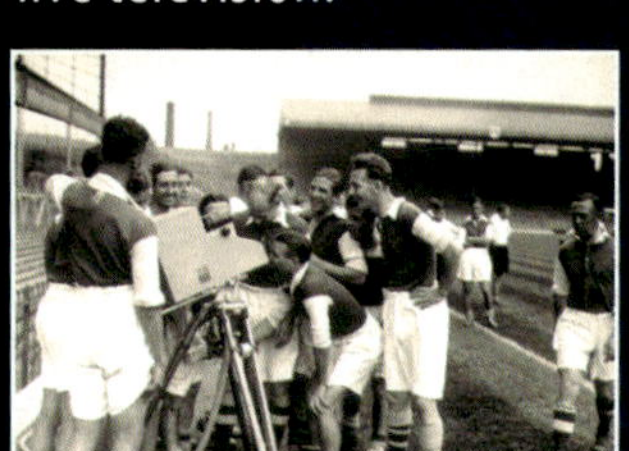

1890 1900 1910 1920 1930 1940 1950

In 1891, Arsenal becomes the first London-based soccer team to turn professional.

1930
Legendary coach Herbert Chapman leads Arsenal to the first league championship in the team's history.

The Future

With some of its talent reaching the end of their club contracts, Arsenal has the potential to gain exciting new players and continue its reign as one of Great Britain's most popular soccer teams. In this age of fan-driven social media, Arsenal's future is the topic of many Twitter and Facebook posts. Only time will tell how the Gunners will fare.

1966

Team physiotherapist Bertie Mee is hired as head coach. Mee would go on to become Arsenal's second-longest serving coach.

2006

Arsenal makes the move to Emirates Stadium, less than 0.5 miles (0.8 kilometers) away, after nearly 100 years at Highbury.

1960 1970 1980 1990 2000 2010 2020

1970

Arsenal wins its first league title in 17 years, ending "The Long Sleep."

In 2004, Arsenal ends a 49-match winning streak, a standing national record, for which they are nicknamed "The Invincibles."

1996

Head coach Arsène Wenger begins a new reign of training, skill development, and championship success for Arsenal.

Write a Biography

Life Story

A person's life story can be the subject of a book. This kind of book is called a biography. Biographies often describe the lives of people who have achieved great success. These people may be alive today, or they may have lived many years ago. Reading a biography can help you learn more about a great person.

Get the Facts

Use this book, and research in the library and on the internet, to find out more about your favorite player. Learn as much about him as you can. What position does he play? What are his statistics in important categories? Has he set any records? Also, be sure to write down key events in the person's life. What was his childhood like? What has he accomplished off the field? Is there anything else that makes this person special or unusual?

Use the Concept Web

A concept web is a useful research tool. Read the questions in the concept web on the following page. Answer the questions in your notebook. Your answers will help you write a biography.

Concept Web

Adulthood

- Where does this individual currently reside?
- Does he or she have a family?

Your Opinion

- What did you learn from the books you read in your research?
- Would you suggest these books to others?
- Was anything missing from these books?

Childhood

- Where and when was this person born?
- Describe his or her parents, siblings, and friends.
- Did this person grow up in unusual circumstances?

Accomplishments off the Field

- What is this person's life's work?
- Has he or she received awards or recognition for accomplishments?
- How have this person's accomplishments served others?

Help and Obstacles

- Did this individual have a positive attitude?
- Did he or she receive help from others?
- Did this person have a mentor?
- Did this person face any hardships?
- If so, how were the hardships overcome?

Accomplishments on the Field

- What records does this person hold?
- What key games and plays have defined his career?
- What are his stats in categories important to his position?

Work and Preparation

- What was this person's education?
- What was his or her work experience?
- How does this person work?
- What is the process he or she uses?

Trivia Time

Take this quiz to test your knowledge of Arsenal FC. The answers are printed upside down under each question.

1 What color are Arsenal's away uniforms?

A. Yellow and blue

2 How many matches did Arsenal go without losing during the 2003–2004 season?

A. 49

3 Which Arsenal head coach asked for an escape clause in his contract?

A. Bertie Mee

4 Which former Arsenal player holds the record for most total goals scored?

A. Thierry Henry

5 How many appearances did David O'Leary make for Arsenal?

A. 722

6 What stadium was home to Arsenal for 93 years?

A. Highbury

7 Who is the longest-serving head coach of Arsenal?

A. Arsène Wenger

8 What is Alexis Sánchez's nickname?

A. "The Wonder Boy"

9 What special gear does Arsenal goalkeeper Petr Čech wear?

A. A helmet

Key Words

club: an athletic team or organization

cups: trophies, and in some cases, the names of actual competitions

defender: also called a back. A player who plays in front of the goal and stops the other team from scoring.

escape clause: a statement in a contract that allows someone to get out of the contract under certain circumstances

forward: a player on a soccer team who normally plays closest to the opponent's goal

goalkeepers: also called goalies. The players responsible for keeping the ball from going into the goal and the only players who are allowed to pick up the ball.

kits: standard attire and equipment worn by soccer players, including shirts, shorts, socks, and shin guards

physiotherapists: medical professionals who treat injuries or issues with exercise or other physical treatments, such as massage

pitch: an area that is used for playing sports

Premier League: England's primary professional league for men's football; was previously called First Division

titles: championships

Index

Bellerín, Héctor 22

Čech, Petr 15, 30
championships 5, 7, 13, 17, 20, 22, 23, 24, 26, 27
Chapman, Herbert 7, 12, 17, 26

Dial Square 7, 26

Emirates Stadium 5, 8, 9, 10, 11, 19, 27

Gooners 19

Henry, Thierry 19, 20, 25, 30
Highbury Stadium 9, 17, 26, 30

Jennings, Pat 21

London, England 4, 5, 7, 11, 20, 21, 26

meat pies 19
Mee, Bertie 17, 27, 30
Mertesacker, Per 23

O'Leary, David 20, 24, 30

Premier League 4, 5, 7, 11, 21, 22, 24

Sánchez, Alexis 4, 23, 30

uniforms 12, 13, 15, 30

Walcott, Theo 22
Wenger, Arsène 5, 7, 16, 17, 20, 27, 30
Wright, Ian 19, 21

Log on to www.av2books.com

AV² by Weigl brings you media enhanced books that support active learning. Go to www.av2books.com, and enter the special code found on page 2 of this book. You will gain access to enriched and enhanced content that supplements and complements this book. Content includes video, audio, weblinks, quizzes, a slide show, and activities.

AV² Online Navigation

Audio
Listen to sections of the book read aloud.

Book Pages
AV² pages directly correspond to pages in the book.

Video
Watch informative video clips.

Embedded Weblinks
Gain additional information for research.

Key Words
Study vocabulary, and complete a matching word activity.

Try This!
Complete activities and hands-on experiments.

Quizzes
Test your knowledge.

Slide Show
View images and captions, and prepare a presentation.

AV² was built to bridge the gap between print and digital. We encourage you to tell us what you like and what you want to see in the future.

Sign up to be an AV² Ambassador at www.av2books.com/ambassador.

Due to the dynamic nature of the Internet, some of the URLs and activities provided as part of AV² by Weigl may have changed or ceased to exist. AV² by Weigl accepts no responsibility for any such changes. All media enhanced books are regularly monitored to update addresses and sites in a timely manner. Contact AV² by Weigl at 1-866-649-3445 or av2books@weigl.com with any questions, comments, or feedback.